# CAT AND BEAR

### Carol Greene · Anne Mortimer

FRANCES LINCOLN

First published in Great Britain in 1998 by
Frances Lincoln Limited, 4 Torriano Mews
Torriano Avenue, London NW5 2RZ

Published by arrangement with Hyperion Books for Children,
New York, New York, USA

ISBN 0-7112-1343-7  hardback
0-7112-1344-5  paperback

The artwork for each picture is prepared using watercolour.
This book is set in 22-point Goudy.

Printed in Singapore

1 3 5 7 9 8 6 4 2

For Tyler and Charlotte
—C. G.

For Alexander, Sam, and Charlie
—A. M.

Bear arrived in a big red box for the Child's birthday.
He was undoubtedly handsome – a fine, sturdy, brown fellow
with a red ribbon around his neck and a twinkle in his eyes.

Cat didn't like Bear at all.

"The Child already has a furry friend," he growled. "Me!
Bear is unnecessary."

Bear twinkled at him.

"Hurray!" said the Child.
"He's lovely."

She hugged Bear and
kissed him on the nose.

"Hmph,"
growled Cat.
"Unnecessary."

But the Child took Bear up to her room
and put him on her bed, in Cat's favourite place
by the pillows. Then she went to eat ice-cream
and birthday cake.

Cat curled up at the foot of the bed and sulked.

Then, suddenly, Cat heard
a gravelly little voice.

*"I like the Child.
I like where I'm at.
But there is something
wrong with that Cat."*

Cat jumped up.
*"You're singing,"*
he hissed. *"Singing!"*

"Only for you.
Only for you.
Bear songs are private,
just for two," sang Bear.

"Outrageous!" snarled Cat.
"Why, you're nothing but an interloper!"

"Interloper anteloper,
riding on a telescoper," sang Bear.

Cat burrowed under the bedspread,
put his paws over his ears,
and went to sleep.
When he woke up again,
he had an idea.

Cats know what to do with
unpleasant things. They bury them.
So Cat knocked Bear over and
pulled the blanket on top of him.

"Mum!" called the Child a little later. "Bear's gone!"

But Mum found Bear right away. That night the Child took him to bed with her.

"Good night, Bear," she said, and she hugged him and kissed him on the nose.

Cat's own nose felt a little lonely. He slept on the chair.

The next morning he had another idea. If he could make the Child stop loving Bear, then she'd love Cat again.

"Now all I need is a clever plan," thought Cat.
He spent all day trying to think of one.

The Child spent all day with Bear.
That evening the Child came upstairs for her bath.
Then she went back downstairs
for her bedtime snack.

As usual she forgot to pull the
plug out of the bath.

And on the edge of the bath
she left Bear.

Splash!

Cat looked into the bath.
"Soggy," he said. "No one loves soggy."
And he strolled into the bedroom.

"Mum!" called the Child a little later. "Bear went swimming and he's all wet."

"Thoroughly soggy," purred Cat.

But then they patted Bear with towels and blow-dried him until he was as good as new.

"You can even have my red ribbon, Bear," said the Child as she snuggled into bed. She hugged Bear and kissed him on the nose.

Cat's own nose felt terrible.

He slept in a corner on the floor.

Then one windy autumn day,
the Child went next door to play.

*"Leaves are falling.*
*Do they care?*
*I would care, but*
*I'm a Bear,"* sang Bear.

Somehow, the Child had left him on the windowsill.

Somehow, she'd left the window open.

And somehow, Bear disappeared

Later, Cat went outside and glanced around.

He couldn't see Bear anywhere.

Wonderful! he thought. Bear ha found himself a new home.

That night the Child missed Bear—a lot.

Cat cuddled up to her and purred. But she sniffled and snuffled until she fell asleep.

Cat himself had trouble sleeping.

He was sure he could hear something.

It was a song, a small, gravelly song.

*"Lost!*
*Alone!*
*Cold!"*

Cat's ears twitched. "Ridiculous!" he said.
But the song came again.

*"Lost! Alone! Cooold!"*

"Just a dream," snorted Cat. "Bear has a new home."
*"Looost!"* came the song yet again. *"Alooone! Sooo cooold!"*

And suddenly Cat felt all those feelings, too. Lost in a dark place that went on forever. Alone in a place where there were no cuddles. Cold – so cold that he shivered.

Cat jumped up. "All Right!" he snarled. "I'm coming."

He padded downstairs and out through his cat-flap.

He stalked to the side of the house and looked beneath the Child's window.

But all he saw there was a prickly bush with leaves heaped around it.

Cat stuck his head under the bush. "No Bear. Back to bed."

But Cat couldn't help sniffing
and he couldn't help smelling,
and all at once he smelled something
deep under the leaves. Something lost
and alone and cold.

"Now I suppose I'll have to DIG," thought Cat.
He dug in the leaves until he finally
dug up a furry brown ear. Then he
grabbed that ear with his teeth
and pulled as hard
as he could.

Out popped Bear.

"I'm *free! I'm free!*
*Oh, come and see.*
*The Noble Cat has rescued me,*"
sang Bear.

    "Has anyone ever
told you that you have a
terrible voice?"
said Cat.

    It was not easy to drag Bear
around the house, and through
the cat-flap, and up all the stairs.

For just a moment, the Child woke up.

"Bear!" she mumbled. "And Cat!"

She hugged them both, kissed their noses, and went back to sleep.

"About time," growled Cat. His nose felt fine.

Then Cat felt Bear take a deep breath.

"*Found!*" sang Bear, and "*Friend!*" and "*Warm!*"

"Hmph," purred Cat.

"Still unnecessary."